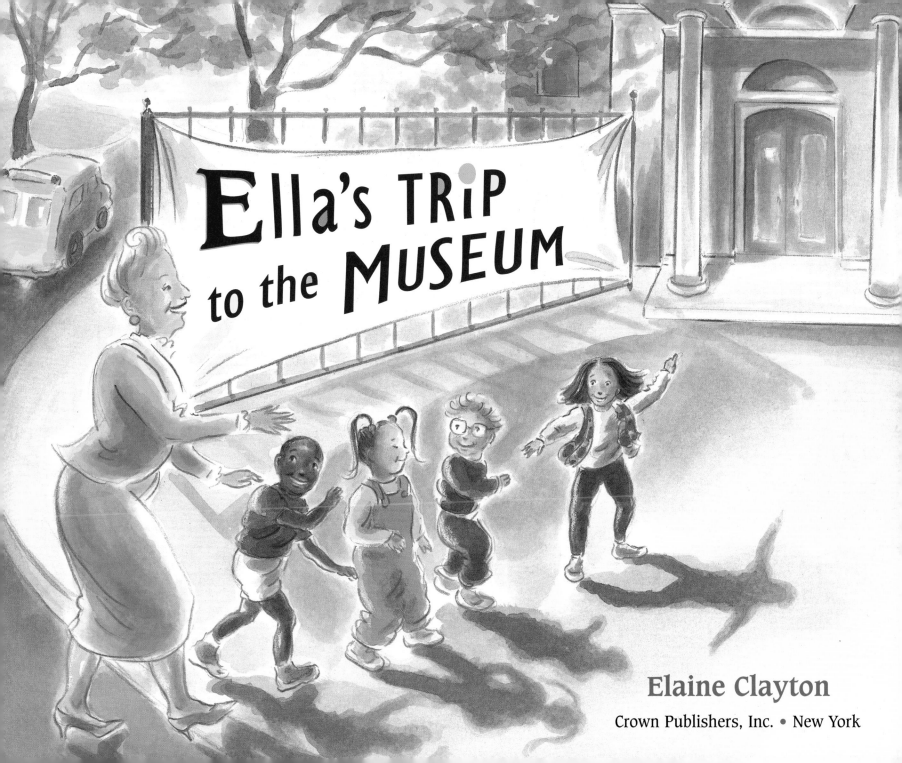

Ella's TRiP to the MUSEUM

Elaine Clayton

Crown Publishers, Inc. • New York

Published by Crown Publishers, Inc., a Random House
company, 201 East 50th Street, New York, NY 10022

CROWN is a trademark of Crown Publishers, Inc.

Manufactured in Singapore

Library of Congress Cataloging-in-Publication Data
Clayton, Elaine.
Ella's trip to the museum / written and illustrated by
Elaine Clayton.
p. cm.
Summary: When Ella visits a museum with her school
group, she shows them how to look at art in a
magical way.
[1. Museums—Fiction. 2. Dancing—Fiction.
3. Statues—Fiction. 4. Magic—Fiction.] I. Title.
PZ7.C57917El, 1996
[E]—dc20   95-18492

ISBN 0-517-70080-8 (trade)
0-517-70081-6 (lib. bdg.)

10 9 8 7 6 5 4 3 2 1

First Edition

*For my former student
who taught me so wel*

When Ella stepped into the museum,

she felt that almost anything could happen.

The teacher, Mrs. Jasper, gave
Ella her puzzled look.

Stay with us, Ella!

Mrs. Jasper took a deep
breath and began the tour.

*Today, children, we will learn
that artists use many different
colors to create special moods.*

I wish I could be a ballerina.

Ella stared at a painting of dancers. She felt the warm glow of the stage lights and heard the rustling of delicate tutus.

The orchestra thundered, and Ella saw
a swirl of pink light all about her.

Meanwhile, Mrs. Jasper reminded the children to look *very carefully* at the painting of dancers.

In this piece, the artist painted shapes and colors to make it look as though the dancers might leap right off the canvas.

Hey! No running or jumping in the museum!

Ella twirled and jumped, leaping as gracefully as she could.

Mrs. Jasper gave Ella her serious look.

These angels were painted in oils.

Ella could not stop staring at the angels.

She heard the swooshing sound of wings
aflutter, and felt a light breeze on her face.

Suddenly, she rose up into a sky of blue and floated on feathery puffs of air!

Ella floated into the next gallery.

*No silly-walking
in the museum!*

Mrs. Jasper gave Ella her worried look.

Stay with us, Ella! I want you to <u>experience</u> the art.

But I am!

Mrs. Jasper led the children into the sculpture gallery.

Now, children, this is a wonderful statue of Flora, the Roman goddess of spring.

Ella stared at Flora. Flora stared back, then looked away.

So Ella pretended *not* to stare.

And that's when

Flora jumped down from her pedestal and taught Ella the dance of spring.

*Absolutely
<u>no</u> dancing
in the museum!*

Ella, where did you get that flower?

From Flora! If you pretend not to stare at her, she'll dance with you!

Mrs. Jasper gave Ella her surprised look.

Nonsense, I'll prove to you that statues do <u>not</u> move.

They stared and waited . . .   and waited and stared . . .

See? Statues do not move.
Now let's go, children.